**Put Beginning Readers on the Right Track with
ALL ABOARD READING™**

The All Aboard Reading series is especially designed for beginning readers. Written by noted authors and illustrated in full color, these are books that children really want to read—books to excite their imagination, expand their interests, make them laugh, and support their feelings. With fiction and nonfiction stories that are high interest and curriculum-related, All Aboard Reading books offer something for every young reader. And with four different reading levels, the All Aboard Reading series lets you choose which books are most appropriate for your children and their growing abilities.

**Picture Readers**

Picture Readers have super-simple texts, with many nouns appearing as rebus pictures. At the end of each book are 24 flash cards—on one side is a rebus picture; on the other side is the written-out word.

**Station Stop 1**

Station Stop 1 books are best for children who have just begun to read. Simple words and big type make these early reading experiences more comfortable. Picture clues help children to figure out the words on the page. Lots of repetition throughout the text helps children to predict the next word or phrase—an essential step in developing word recognition.

**Station Stop 2**

Station Stop 2 books are written specifically for children who are reading with help. Short sentences make it easier for early readers to understand what they are reading. Simple plots and simple dialogue help children with reading comprehension.

**Station Stop 3**

Station Stop 3 books are perfect for children who are reading alone. With longer text and harder words, these books appeal to children who have mastered basic reading skills. More complex stories captivate children who are ready for more challenging books.

In addition to All Aboard Reading books, look for All Aboard Math Readers™ (fiction stories that teach math concepts children are learning in school) and All Aboard Science Readers™ (nonfiction books that explore the most fascinating science topics in age-appropriate language).

All Aboard for happy reading!

To my little princess, Molly Rose—D.H.

To Steven James Petruccio,
whose artistic assistance on this book
is greatly appreciated—N.C.

Text copyright © 1996 by Deborah Hautzig. Illustrations copyright © 1996 by Natalie Carabetta.
All rights reserved. Adapted from Frances Hodgson Burnett's *A Little Princess*. Published by
Grosset & Dunlap, a division of Penguin Putnam Books for Young Readers, 345 Hudson Street,
New York, NY 10014. ALL ABOARD READING and GROSSET & DUNLAP are trademarks of
Penguin Putnam Inc. Published simultaneously in Canada. Printed in the U.S.A.

*Library of Congress Cataloging-in-Publication Data*

Hautzig, Deborah.
    A little princess / by Deborah Hautzig ; illustrated by Natalie Carabetta.
      p.    cm. — (All aboard reading. Level 3)
    "Adapted from Frances Hodgson Burnett's A little princess."
    Summary: Sara Crewe, a pupil at Miss Minchin's London school, is left in poverty when
her father dies but is later rescued by a mysterious benefactor.
    [1. Boarding schools—Fiction.   2. Schools—Fiction.   3. Orphans—Fiction.   4. London
(England)—Fiction.]   I. Carabetta, Natalie, ill.   II. Burnett, Frances Hodgson, 1849-1924.
Little princess.   III. Title.   IV. Series.
PZ7.H2888Li  1996
[E]—dc20                                      96-22426
                                             CIP
                                           AC

ISBN 0-448-41327-2          I J

ALL ABOARD READING™

Station Stop
3

# A Little Princess

**Adapted from Frances Hodgson Burnett's**
*A Little Princess*
**By Deborah Hautzig**
**Illustrated by Natalie Carabetta**

**Grosset & Dunlap • New York**

On a dark winter day in London, Sara Crewe sat in a cab with her father.

Usually, Sara was happy. But not now. Her father was going far away.

"Papa," said Sara, cuddling close to him, "can't you stay with me at Miss Minchin's school?"

Her father smiled sadly. "No, my dear. I must go back to India—and it is better for you to be here."

When they came to the school, Miss Minchin was waiting. She had cold, fishy eyes and a fishy smile. Sara wanted to like her, but it was hard.

"Sara's happiness means the world to me," Captain Crewe said. "She must have everything she wants."

Miss Minchin's eyes gleamed. She knew Captain Crewe was very rich. "Of course," she said. "Come, I will take you to Sara's room."

Sara's room was cheerful and lovely. Lace curtains fluttered in all the windows. There were shelves filled with storybooks, and many beautiful dolls to play with.

After Miss Minchin had gone, Sara sat on her father's lap and touched his face.

"Are you learning me by heart?" he said gently.

"No, I know you by heart. You are inside my heart," said Sara. She kissed him good-bye.

The next day, Sara met her school-mates. Everyone had heard about Sara.

"She has a maid and a pony and boxes of fancy dresses," whispered Lavinia. "Miss Minchin says it is silly for a child to have so much."

"Girls, you must welcome Sara Crewe," said Miss Minchin. "Sara, sit by me."

Lavinia turned red with anger. "Sara is sitting in my place!" she hissed.

Lavinia was mean and bullied the younger girls. But before Sara came, Lavinia had been the "star pupil."

Now Sara walked at Miss Minchin's side. She was a "star," but she was never nasty. Sara was always kind and giving.

The other girls were enchanted by Sara. She made up such wonderful stories! Every day they gathered round to hear Sara tell about kings and princesses and fairies and mermaids.

Sometimes Sara saw Becky, the servant girl, listening. Miss Minchin was forever scolding Becky, and Becky was very fearful and shy. Sara spoke a little louder. That way Becky could hear, too.

"She's a girl just like me," Sara said to herself. "And stories belong to everyone."

Sara wanted to know more about Becky. One day she got her chance. She walked into her room and found Becky fast asleep.

"Poor thing!" she cried softly. "She works so hard." She waited quietly until Becky woke up.

"Oh, miss!" cried Becky. "Please pardon me!"

"Don't be afraid," said Sara. "We are just the same—I am a little girl, like you. Can you stay and have some cake with me?"

Becky's hungry eyes grew huge. Cake!

"Oh, yes, miss—thank you!" she said.

The next few minutes seemed like a dream to Becky. Sara was so nice to her.

"Once I saw a princess," Becky told Sara. "You look just like her."

"Sometimes I pretend I am a princess," Sara said. "I make up stories about it. One day I'll tell them to you."

"Oh, miss!" said Becky. "Stories are even better than cake!"

Sara knew just what Becky meant.

A week before her birthday, Sara got an exciting letter. It was from her father.

Captain Crewe had a friend who owned diamond mines. The friend had asked Captain Crewe to be his partner. Sara's father would be even richer now—a man of fortune!

That wasn't all. "You must have a special birthday," wrote Captain Crewe. "I have told Miss Minchin to give you a huge party."

And what a party it was! Every room
was hung with holly and colored
balloons. There were six different kinds
of cakes. A table was piled high with gifts.

"Thank you all for coming to my party," said Sara, feeling a bit shy.

"Very nice, Sara," said Miss Minchin. "You behave like a real princess."

Suddenly, Miss Minchin was called away from the party. A visitor had news for her.

A few minutes later, Miss Minchin
returned. She had a hard look on her face.

"The party is over!" she shouted. "Go
to your rooms. Not you, Sara."

Now Sara was alone with Miss
Minchin.

"Your father is dead," Miss Minchin
said coldly.

Sara did not make a sound. Her eyes
got big, and she turned pale.

"He left no money at all," Miss
Minchin told her. "You are not a princess
anymore. You are a beggar. You must
work for a living. Now, go to the attic.
You will sleep there, next to Becky."

But when Sara turned to leave, Miss
Minchin said, "Stop! Aren't you going to
thank me for my kindness? I am giving
you a home!"

Sara lifted her chin. It shook a little.

"You are not kind," she said fiercely.
"And this is not a home!"

Sara slowly climbed the stairs to the attic. When she opened the door, her heart fell.

It was the saddest room she had ever seen. The paint was peeling. There was a hard bed and a shabby little stool. Cold ashes filled the fireplace. The dirty window looked out on the house next door. It was dark and empty.

Sara began to cry. "My papa is dead," she said over and over.

There was a soft tap at the door.

Becky came in. She had been crying, too.

"I'm so sorry for you, miss!" she said.

Sara tried to stop her tears.

"You see, Becky," she said bravely. "I told you we were the same—just two little girls. I'm not a princess anymore."

Becky threw her arms around Sara.

"Yes, you are, miss," she said. "You will always be a princess!"

Sara's new life was horrible. She worked and scrubbed and cleaned from morning until night.

Most of the girls felt sorry for her. But not Lavinia. She loved to watch as "Princess Sara" cleaned her room. She always found extra work for Sara to do.

"Bring me more coal for the fire. <u>My</u> father can pay for it," snapped Lavinia. "Those shelves look dusty. Clean them again. Then you may polish my shoes." Sara quietly did as she was told.

Sara was sent out in the rain and the snow to do chores for Miss Minchin. All she had to wear was a thin coat and old, worn-out shoes. She shivered with cold. She never had enough to eat, so she was always hungry.

But Sara never complained.

"I have to be brave, like a real princess," she told herself. "Papa would want that. And I can pretend that I am warm and full and happy. Pretending makes everything better."

Every night, Sara told Becky stories.
Sometimes the stories were about them.

"Our room is so high, it is like a cozy nest," Sara said. "Pretend there is a soft rug. And a hot fire, and a shelf full of books. And a table with tea and cakes. And a big soft bed with silk covers. Think of it!"

"Oh, miss!" Becky would say. "How lucky we are to be here!"

Because when Sara told it, it felt real.

Sara looked out her window one evening and saw lights. People were living in the house next door! Who were they?

Finally, Sara saw someone, but it wasn't a person. It was a little monkey! He sat chattering by the window. Suddenly the monkey leaped across the roof to Sara's window, and jumped onto Sara's head! Sara laughed with delight.

Seconds later, an Indian gentleman came chasing after the monkey. His name was Ram Dass. He looked in Sara's window.

"Come back, you bad monkey!" he scolded. But he smiled as he said it.

By now the monkey was racing
around the attic. After a short chase, he
jumped into Sara's arms. Sara handed
him to Ram Dass.

"Thank you, miss," said Ram Dass.
"My master will be so grateful! He is
always sad, and the monkey makes him
laugh."

"Why is he sad?" asked Sara.

"His best friend died," said Ram Dass. "And now he is looking for his friend's child. He will not rest until he finds her."

"I'm sorry," said Sara. "I hope your master finds the child."

Ram Dass took the monkey home, and told his master all about Sara.

"She lives in such a cold, awful room," said Ram Dass. "It is no place for a little girl."

That night, Sara went to bed hungry and cold, as usual. But when she woke up, she was warm and cozy. She reached out and felt a satin blanket.

"I must be dreaming," she said. Then she opened her eyes. "This can't be real!" she gasped.

But it was. A thick rug lay on the
floor. There was a glowing fire and a
table covered with food. A silk robe and
slippers lay waiting for her. A pile of
books lay nearby. On top was a note: "To
the little girl in the attic. From a friend."

Sara ran to get Becky. "It's magic!" she cried. "A magician came while we were sleeping!"

The two girls sat by the fire. They had fruit and muffins and tea.

"Will it all melt away?" asked Becky.

"No," said Sara. "I pinched myself to be sure it is real."

The girls didn't expect the magic to happen again. But from then on, every morning and every night, a cheery fire and a hot meal waited for them.

Sara still worked hard. Miss Minchin was nastier than ever. But Sara did not mind. She had a secret friend. She only wished that somehow she could say thank you.

One day, the monkey came back.

"You silly thing!" said Sara. She hid him under her coat and slipped next door.

"You found our monkey again!" said Ram Dass when he saw her. "Please come in. The master, Mr. Carrisford, will be glad if you visit."

Inside sat a sad-looking man with a kind face.

"So you're the little girl in the attic," said Mr. Carrisford.

Suddenly, Sara understood.

"You sent those wonderful things to me," she said slowly. "<u>You</u> are my friend!" She took his thin hand and kissed it.

"Tell me, what is your name?" asked Mr. Carrisford.

"Sara," she said. "Sara Crewe."

Mr. Carrisford became so pale, Sara was afraid he would faint.

"What's wrong?" she cried.

"You are Captain Crewe's child," said Mr. Carrisford in wonder. "He was my best friend. I have been looking for you for so long!"

"I am the child you were looking for?" Sara whispered. "And I was right next door!"

"If only I had known," Mr. Carrisford said. "You see, Sara, your father did not lose his fortune. I have kept it for you. You will live a good life with me."

"I'm glad," said Sara. "But please, what about Becky? She lives in the attic, too, and Miss Minchin is so mean to her!"

"Becky can come, too," said Mr. Carrisford.

The very same day, Sara and Becky left Miss Minchin's school forever. Miss Minchin was angry and upset. She even begged Sara to come back! But Sara said, "Never."

Most of the girls were happy for Sara. Becky, of course, was happiest of all.

"I was right," Becky told Sara. "You always were a princess. You always will be."

"I always tried to be," Sara said softly.